Sentinels

Fireflies of the Gardens

S. Jefferson

pencil

ISBN 978-93-5667-514-8
© S. Jefferson 2023
Published in India 2023 by Pencil

A brand of

One Point Six Technologies Pvt. Ltd.
123, Building J2, Shram Seva Premises,
Wadala Truck Terminal, Wadala (E)
Mumbai 400037, Maharashtra, INDIA
E connect@thepencilapp.com
W www.thepencilapp.com

Author biography

My name is Jefferson Silva Pinho de Jesus, I was born on February 22, 1998, I am 24 years old.

I graduated at the age of 16 in a public high school, at the same time I had already graduated

in English and studied graphic design, I have always been a lover of art and also of the health field,

when I graduated in design, after a while I entered the pharmacy course and before finishing the course,

published an academic article on the pandemic, I won a dance contest in the genre of street dance.

Today I live by the poems of life, by the words that make the hearts swings.

CONTENTS

Epigraph

There is no brightness without shadow, even the purest light is accompanied by a mist that haunts it... because lightness invites darkness to ascend, and darkness accepts the call of brightness.

Acknowledgements

I thank the lights of my life, the companions of my path, who supported the clarity of my plot, became the foundation of my writing. All support, no matter how it is, is welcome, the humanity, the affection, the reception and I thank everyone, I would be nothing without the brilliance of those who support me.

The Rise of Shining Sentinel

Sentinels are not born Sentinels, they become Sentinels. The mission they carry, without even knowing it, makes them vigilant.

I do not know who I am... plunged into the depths of my darkness, unable to distinguish what is outside from what is inside, a place of visible silence, having invisible inner chaos, being me, devoid of my own qualities, carried along a lost path of shadows. The abyss retains all positivity, I am as deep as a root can reach, connected to the hidden where only dark exists, trapped, I have become part of abyss, as if I don't exist, the only thing I know is my rottenness, I am an abyss and abyss is me and that's all there is in me, it's as if I don't really live completely, I only have this dark and this dark have me.

The Guardians of Light are only awake when they are shining, so before illuminate they don't know who are, just a dark matter in the deepest that can exist.

I only remember the deep feelings, so deep they are beyond my heart, they only remember that darkness, can feelings be so strong? I am out of control, my intensity has consumed all structures, structures of qualities, feelings that possess me, fetters reducing the soul and enlarging my ego, I am just another repulsive part of the insensitive nature, insensitive for being always alone, loneliness is what accompanies me in the storms of my ego.

Before to be what they should be, they must shatter, Sentinels are surges of light as well as resurrections of bran and ash, must give up what they are now to be.

Everything unpleasant in me was attracted, trying to come together, similar to a shattered glass now struggling to reassemble itself, parts affected by deviation of its own virtues, my nature broken, crumpled, and the darkness used to shatter, I came close to being in bran, but my pieces now want to reunite, the only phenomenon fitted in a face of so many detachments, I am more detached than a key that does not belong to a lock, though it goes in, but is unable to open it.

They have to walk in a path to discover yourselves, vigilant are the walkers who bring clarity with them, there is still much to know about.

Time passed, and I became weaker and weaker, because I did not understand myself. Storms of chaos changed itself, chose a form that wanted to take me, pushed away the dark clouds and the fog that surrounded me. Now I have only myself and nothing else, although I already felt alone, even with darkness as my companion. Everything can leave me one day, including who I am, to be better I need to abandon myself, since the darkness left? Darkness devoured me and when I changed it left me, so I'll transform myself to triumph over the confrontations of life. It is impossible to abandon myself, but I can enlighten my ego.

To be light you have to transform the darkness, but darkness is not completely formed and light too, one needs the other, one part has to shine, and the other has to darken.

I was ennobled by my changes, I never thought that I would overcome myself in the face of my confusions. My emptiness decided to split, the transformations in my inner self revealed the light to my outer self, an accumulation of misunderstandings that were understood, transformed into light, I began to understand myself, I needed the darkness to lead me to the light. That enlightenment is showing a way, although I do not know where I am going, I follow a radiant path that reveals itself to me, I am traveling as if it were light, shining through the combustion of obscurity. I had to awaken my spirit that was drowned in my negligence, it made me change.

It is a long journey to become unobscured, and even if they succeed, they still have darkness to live through.

II will never allow myself to be completely invaded again, I was weakened by improper nature, not understanding what is wonderful for me. In fact, I asked to be completely hidden in order to find who I am, but was it really necessary? For the first time my ego allowed lights to emerge within me, allowed myself to be shaped by the turbulence of my being, it felt important to leave myself to find myself. The sparkle that now shines is enough to make me feel alive. My connection to a night is internal, different from outside. I am myself and night is night. I am part of the abyss, but I am not it.

Foz & Algoz

There is something driving me, like a voice that doesn't speak, a part of me that I don't know? I keep wandering in the night, left, right, up or down, sometimes I forget who is who, which is north or south, one part of me has met while the other has missed, where am I going? Remaining in the abyss, believing that I will get out of it, since there is something trying to take me where I never went. Will I finally discover myself there? It is strange to be a firefly that only fly, a talking light that only talks, my dialogue is only with myself. Feeling like in an alley and there are no exits in the alleys, but there is a voice whispering: when there are no exits, break the barriers and make openings, the openings are paths. Maybe opening up, letting my light expand is a way out of all this, am I still afraid of my hidden self? Of the capacity of the parts I will strip away?

After struggling with self-ego for fear of what was inside me, I decided to open up, if before I was imprisoned by the abyss, today I am handcuffed to my enlightenment, and right now I will dissolve this chain, doors will fall, barriers will collapse. So I did, unlocking all my locks, concentrating, allowing my brightness to unleash itself in a flash, radiating its own luminosity, feeling like a star, an irrepressible meteor. The light spread out in all directions, at that moment I saw many paths opening up, and in one of them the brightness stopped for a while, going towards the sky, towards what is above me, in small particles. Once again, the voice spoke to me: Follow a path of light that rises up to the heavens. In spite of everything I saw myself empty, weakened, all my luminosity about to cease, my own broken radiance beginning to fail, am I... a firefly about to die?

Cells, which were lamps, wanted to go out, and I, without being aware of such a fact, had no hope, since the luminosity brought it to me, but I remember this voice that spoke to me moments ago, perhaps it is my hope now. Even though I constituted myself in total darkness, I remind well where the luminous fragments rose. I continued on this path, overcoming my feelings of pain and loss, believing that one day my determination would prevail.

After some time... I'm already tired of wandering.

I don't know how much time has passed. I am like a lightwander, moving without legs, but I see, the vision of light still enlarges, but nothing is visible beyond an abyss that exists outside and inside me. The chaos favors the urge of darkness to aspire to whatever hope was left.

After a long time I saw a luminous field, I have never seen anything like it, like an orbit, approaching and illuminating me, my negative judgments became silent with so much light until its brightness faded. The sphere said:

— Lightwatcher, your sparklife, a great ember, has fallen asleep. I am aware of the time it will take for you to be reborn, so I will take care of your needs and give you my bright. We, the watchful lights, gives bright and inhale the hopeless, so never give your light completely, lest only darkness remain.

— Who introduces himself? How could you not confuse me with this abyss? What is sparklife?

— My name is Axanar, which means magister, baptized by the lightwatcher of long nights, the expert of bright, and he called me master, and when we met I found myself immature, just like you. I nominate you as Prosopher, the one who receives and gives flashes of light, Because even when I am far away, I can see your luminosity. His sparklife is something you must take care of, it is in the deepest part of his being.

— Not even I see this light that you said, in what way did you notice it?

— Darkness and light dwell in all beings, even if your darkness is exposed, see the glow emanating from within you, believe in yourself. — said Axanar.

I was stunned by all the things that had happened, and I did not have the time to react, much less digest what had been said.

Axanar conjured his glow as my darkness came to him, I saw my self-balancing, intended that shadow and clarity were in perfect equifinality. I made it clear that I didn't comprehend much, that I knew little about myself, about what I would do once balanced. He said:

— It is still early. I needed to come at you, because where you "step" you have to see, long nights hide many things, but the eye-bright will guide you, even in the existence of many layers, you will see. Go and remember your journey of giving to those in need. You are a Sentinel as well as, shun being a Phagonela, they feed on the glare, and we give it away, feeding on the darkness, making it an illumination. Follow your path. — hoped with words.

When I began to interpret my processes, I followed where needed to go, everything got clear, walking in a path that became a way out of the abyss, now I am in the forest of human world, with many fireflies, Sentinels like me, wandering around trees, grass, animals, people, each other, mutually, as they did with me. Axanar cured me of the dark fever, lower imbalance of my inner nature. The excess of light brought me back to darkness, an abuse of the pitch itself made me as similar to abyss, but thanks to the balance it gave me, I know what to do from now on.

— Glittering spheres have no eyes, but they glitter by entering into the depths; therefore, they see with lights like eyes, the eye-bright, the iris of bright. — words from one Sentinel to another—heard Prosopher when he arrived in the world.

My eyes have changed, in fact they are not eyes but rays of light that give a deep vision, I see beyond appearances, I see shadows that hide, observing the light that does not shine, there are shadows that cannot be seen from the outside, because they are hidden from the inside, light that does not shine, but bright in essence, in the hearts, Some spread light without shining too brightly, preferring to shine even in their own darkness, They are Sentinels like me, sentinels illuminated by their attitude, and the Phagonellas suck energy and obscure the light of others, It is easier to use someone else's brightness to benefit itself than to shine, but happy lights bright for those in need without asking for anything in return, and this path that I will follow, the shared brightness will also be mine, this is more than enough, it will become greater and humbler.

There are small things that are inhumble, and humility does not see greatness, for it is glimpsed by character.

I see some flowers that despair when it gets dusky, they are afraid of the dark, if they only knew what I have experienced... Sunflowers love the sun and even at night they refuse my light.

They believe that only brightness of the sun is enough, they have no notion that large doses are bad for them, because one hour it runs out, having to deal with the consequence of excess, sunflowers are addicted to light, this is sad, I hope to be able to help them one day. I found flowers close to wilting, crying out for help to the watchers, are too many and our light has a very limited range. If I do as before, it is possible to lose the shine, So one must have self-control to help without harming oneself. As I approached, noticed that there were elements of darkness surrounding them, and when I went to conjure my light intending to retain the negativity, something appeared next to me: two obscured orbits, which originated from the negative events in the flowers. These spheres phagocytosed my energy, slowly depleted the luminosity, until there was nothing left, causing me a second dark fever. The doom of my characteristics consolidated again, misunderstandings grew, chaos became what I was when I didn't want to be, my inexperience in the world.

I fought to put my pieces together, I fought to understand the darkness, to be facing haunts that inhabit me, fevers are natural. I must learn from the fever of my soul, not just from my lamp's glaze.

Not only that, but I have finally managed to soften my own wracks, discovered that it is possible to be in the dark without losing control, but it is a fervent conflict.

Fever, as my perception allows, grant knowledge of the occult, of things that not even my lamps have revealed to me. I understood that I was just like them, was born a Phagonela to be a sentinel, it is strange to recognize my transformation, but it was necessary, and now I have become the same when I was born, a negligent of chaos, a Phagonela. Thought my essence made of darkness, then I changed, believed that brilliance belonged to me, and in fact my nature still inappropriate, having to be light-dark, the equalization of intern aspects.

Although I have conquered the darkness, it always comes back to fight.

It is a constant effort, one hour I win, the next I lose, and at this very moment it crushes me, can't stay in the darkness for long.

I have held on as long as I can... even so, there is still much to understand about myself, however, I must learn to deal fully with the darkness.

I stopped hiking to clutter, the absorption of flicker slows down the natural processes, exhausting the genuine order of things, I thought the Phagonellas just drained energy from the Sentinels, being me, one of them, my thirst was for any light that might shine. My eyesight narrowed, from losing the lights when I got perverted, and yet any brightness I could see, even if it stays on the other side of mountain. The lights draw us in, the luminance calls the darkness back to brilliance, and even if it invites, we are too deaf to hear its call, the silence of our aspects coming from the darkness within. I ask myself in what way can I sip the brightness of everything without becoming light again?

Guided by the hunger of the darkness to find the glow, I'm camouflaged near the luminous wanderers. The darkness that dwells stirred, protruding into me, trying to extend itself into the armlike lightwatchers, similar a murky mist, and I weak to resist, perhaps, lose my sanity to the darkness.

— Out of the obscurity the lights spring—whispers.

Suddenly, after hearing the whisper, I felt reluctant, which gave me some strength, I resisted... and just as I was about to surrender, the darkness faded, I see a lightwatcher giving his life, saving me from the shadows. He enlightened, and the chaos equalized, but this Sentinel came up short, and now my corruptions pervert him. I, who shine now, conjure a glow in him, balancing us, making us more and more alike, as Axanar did, but we are two weakly lights.

— The Phagonellas are saved by the lights retaining their gloom

— I owe you much of my light. What is your name? — asked Prosopher.

— I am Aesus, who gives direction to the lost — said.

— Thanks to you, my mission can be continued.

— thanked Prosopher.

— I prefer to get lost than allow the Sentinels, like you, to be lost by it, the disorder. —said Aesus.

— I understand your devotion, and although I do not have the same experience as you, I ask you to understand what I will say, spending time in dark has taught me how to be light. If you are consumed, the vigilant trait can be disposed of, You will turn out to be negligent because of the chaos. In what ways can you help those in need? — questioned Prosopher.

— That's what the mission of the Sentinels is. To live for light even if we transmuted in chaos. — affirmed Aesus.

— Once I was told: "I had to come to you, for you must see where you "step", I was baptized as one who gives brightness, because I was given luminosity, and we balanced each other out, so I did the same for you, for what you did to me. When you neared, your luminosity was humiliated by your own services, as watch-lamps we need to recharge ourselves, or we will be charged by the storms of neglect. Be a lamp that looks at itself before shining on another. — advised Prosopher.

— You're right, your wisdom enchants me, your lamps of life are insurmountable. I've lived most of the time serving the woodlands, I've forgotten myself. Let me be your Foz? — Aesus asked.

— Foz? What would that be? — asked Prosopher.

— The Foz is the union of two or more Sentinels, they become stronger when they are connected, the Foz is the shape of love, is the sweet and healthy nature of the united, that will be more than allied. There is no word that fits what the Foz means. — said Aesus.

— After your accomplishments, I would accept anything good coming from you, I recognize that we have much to learn together. — acknowledged Prosopher.

— Phagonelas also gather., strengthening their empires, fertilizing their tormentors, powerful beasts of darkness that drain the lights. We are armed against chaos when we unite our torches. — said Aesus.

Clarendel

When we metamorphosed as one, my constitution grew larger, Aesus turned into a small wandering light surrounding me, and I into a voluminous radiation. We were two lights, peregrine, as one, we discuss, we share memories, is incredible, no longer feeling alone, we developed like a guiding ray, with many Sentinels following us. Where we passed by, got whitish, due to strength of lightning. We are a sun walking on earth, say forests and sunflowers about us.

Many sunflowers have been healed by a glow so similar to sun, but which controls its brightness so as not to drench them in light. Together, we acted, Aesus directed me where I had to go, we lit up several gardens while it was night, sunflowers learned not to absorb too much light, to have a little illumination at night. We keep moving, the plants, the flowers, the trees, all the beings we met were enchanted by our brilliance, the gardens stopped clamoring, the negligent, even though they were already living in hiding, hid themselves from our presence. The only time that our brilliance stops is when the sun appears, so much light, when it is close to dawn, the luminescence weakens, we, as well those of all Sentinels, recharge their bright in the presence of the greatest luminary of the day.

We interpret, then, that work in this region has been completed, the number of lightwatchers has grown, for having converted them to equilibrium, Would that be our moment to rest?

— I feel you, Aesus, so comforting, still and calm, just as I saw you the first time, quieting my embarrassments. Do you want to rest? — realized Prosopher.

— Even with rest at dawn, for expressing so much light, at night I get down. — said Aesus.

— Contemplating of your same weariness, should we rest a few nights? — asked Prosopher.

— I get nervous about resting when we should be shining. Chaos always waits for a crack in order to disarrange. — expressed Aesus.

— Let our light be renewed at night to illuminate better. Do not worry, for nothing ever rests, only when it perishes. — answered Prosopher.

— Because both need a repose, I will accept the laziness in some evenings. — said Aesus.

We kept ourselves in a tree trunk for the first time, going out only to receive the rays of the great luminary of day and night, some evenings, we stayed in the trunk when the moon was ashamed, at the moment she hides, the phagonellas have more chances to omit our lights.

Everything proceeded in perfect normality on the first night, only the sunflowers asked for our return, but they were content with the watchers lamps, even though they were not very bright. On the second day everyone noticed our absence, and we wanted to shine, but still preferred to receive brilliance of the moon and sun, improving our sparkle. Since we went two, which is also only one, needed more time to refuel, Neither were we fully charged by charging with them. Any light that shines too brightly discharges itself excessively, yes, we are discharged by our brightness, So we repose to not be victims of negligence, of the weakening within light itself.

On the fifth day we noticed stirrings at dawn, branches of the tree moved like arms, they stretched further into the short opening in the trunk, opening it even more, we suspected that the tree wanted to be alone.

— I was tortured last night. You should be doing your duty. — complained the tree.

— Who or what tortures you? — asked Foz.

— Your opponents. They withered my leaves, even masked they can find the presence of fireflies, you attracted them. We trees ensured the clarity by our foliage, and now what am I going to do? — asked the tree.

— We will go out, and our brightness will dispel the chaos, you shall see the integrity of yourself again. — said Aesus.

— You rested for so long that you didn't realize the narrow things coming — said the tree.

As we left the tree there were several Phagonellas, just as, light leads to darkness, darkness leads to light, there were Sentinels too, all the way around, the glow we carried made the chaotic-neglects move away and the clarity of the Sentinels was restored, The leaves that we lay the ray were regenerated through our sharing of goodness with them. As we shine, the unenlightenment, eventually departs.

— The vigilant concentrated on watching the flowers and helping the Phagonellas, but they forgot the trees, we live too, we suffer, in fact it was the first time I spoke to the

Watchers. So you are the restoration of the world, the justice of love and kindness. I give you the power of the branches, you will regenerate yourselves even if there is no light, You are no longer dependent on the moon or the sun, but on time, for everything that needs to be healed has its time to heal. — explained the tree.

The branches and leaves surrounded us, turning into a great tangle, some entered us, ended up being transformed into luminosity, the tangle unraveled. Aesus grew like a rose clutching its own light, and that light is me.

— What will be our thanks to you? — Aesus asked.

— Most beautiful rose of gardens, heal the pain that has spread through the woods, aid the discharmonious voices that cry out for help, and will see that you are not just a rose. That's a way to be grateful. — replied the tree.

All the trees, seeing our apotheosis, marveled, heroized us, the roots lifted our spirits, and countless branches from the middle of the forest turned toward us, we are now the Cyrus of the Forest, is the name they gave us. The things that were destabilized when we were resting have been restored, the sunflowers are healthy, all the Phagonelas have left for other lands, the moon is no longer shy in this place, evenings are similar to dawning, the lightwatchers arround us singing: the Cyrus of the garden, it brought me happiness, the peace of tiny brights.

We took care of the vegetations, the mud, everyone who lived there, and still I, who knew little about everything, asked: how did you know about Foz Aesus?

— Sentinels teach Sentinels when they are Phagonellas. I had only one dark fever, and the one who saved me said I must be Foz for my light has always been weak. The negligent of chaos cares little for thin lights, thanks to which I was able to save many who were lost. We don't need to shine much to do good things, but we must reach out to those who overwhelm our brightness. Watchers repel watchers and attract Phagonellas. That's why I knew we belonged together, that we were committed to shining in the same way, with the same intensity, without repelling each other, maybe the watchers repuls themselves since they shine with unequal intensities. — Aesus answered clearly.

— When I saw you, when we were equal, I realized that your bright, even though it is weak, was enough for me, that I didn't need much to be prosopher. I have spent times alone, in the dark, in the world, and today knew a companion takes the loneliness from my heart. Aesus, my Foz. — Spoke Prosopher with affection.

All the fireflies saw us as The Wise Cyrus, and the trees provided us as Cyrus of the Forest. In gratitude to the trees, we radiated light through branches and roots, their leaves turned brights, to the flowers we were a lamp and their petals revived in luminescence, and to the Sentinels we shared our knowledge. Many tried to match their light in an attempt to be Foz, but could barely connect, others remembered the trees and went to heal our brightness could not reach, we are the Luminous Forest.

— We are joyful, great by our humbleness, rich by impoverishing the ego and enriching the soul, we are the light of personality, guardians of the gardens. — said The Wise Cyrus to lightwatchers.

A new thought was propagated by us, the Cyrus: Watchers are the brightness of a personality, watchers are the development of one's own balanced characteristics, the equifinality between brightness and shadow, although it is difficult, many imagine it to be equifinality.

— We will all dispel the shadows that exist in the world, and nightfall will be like the dawn through the presence of fireflies and the light that guides us. — said Cyrus in the Luminous Garden.

Aesus and I call ourselves "the guiding light" because we give directions to the watchers through understanding our functions.

Suddenly a Sentinel came and said:

— Why can't I unite with another?

— For you shine in different intentions. It's hard to be like others, each of us is unique, so bright with others that shine like you, not the same, but similar. — Aesus replied.

He thanked and left.

After many bright evenings, Aesus asked me:

— Shall we go out and watch?

— We can't leave our pedestal, or the forest will think we are ungrateful. — said Prosopher.

— I don't think we need to go out, we'll just tell the fireflies to keep watch at the edge of garden.

— replied Aesus with other idea.

— I agree with you, although I am curios about our reasons for the vigil. — asked Prosopher.

— Remember that light invites darkness to a banquet. — Aesus advised.

— I will request it. Once again, you remain wise to the onslaught of chaos. — replied Prosopher, recognizing Aesus' qualities.

Then Cyrus decided to inform everyone with the breeze of his rumors:

— Fireflies, you light up the garden, but there is no happiness that lasts forever. I ask you to use your lamps in the woods, where the trees still have their dark leaves. Whoever does good should not stop doing good. — said Cyrus.

Everyone spread out into the glowing forest, while Cyrus searched for answers through the trees that clung to him with their branches.

— Where are the devourers of the wood's mother sparks? — asked Prosopher.

— They are looking for new floras, the fire of the lightwatchers has made them hungry. — said the tree.

After making the observation, they returned without noticing the involvement of darkness in the woods. The trees became suspicious:

— Though none of us, nor the guards, have noticed any unwelcome presence. A Sentinel has yet to return. — said one of the trees.

— Has he perverted himself? — Foz asked worriedly.

— We don't know. The carelessness of the trunk makes weeds grow. Be careful! — warned the tree.

— We appreciate your guidance, wise tree. — said Foz.

— I am the oldest tree in the Luminous Garden, and the same one that gave you apotheosis, I encourage the others to do the same. — empha sized the tree.

— That's why you will be our guide tree. Help us take care of the park where the watchers usually floats. — Cyrus asked. (Cyrus and Foz are the same).

Everyone continued to be cheerful, some remained in their mission to keep watch, and there were still those who tried to participate, everything in motion, lamps going from one side to the other, lights up our backyard and make it shine. When we least expected it, a Sentinel accosted us from a distance where it would not be fended off.

— Satisfaction for my rodeo. I had to go beyond the limits to find what could not be found. — said.

— Is something disturbing the joy of the lights? — asked Prosopher.

— From trunk to trunk, I moved away from the comfortable, and the farther I went, the darker it became. We live in only a small part of a great thing, the careless are close to our limits, they have carried the weight of dark, and they're hungry for our lights. The neighboring courtyards are out of balance, many guardians have been taken over by shadows. The wood of trees allowed me to return, they were the bulwark of the obscurity that took possession of me. — said the Sentinel.

— If we send the guardians there? — Aesus asked.

— The guards will be devoured by them, they are more than the watch-lights that are here.— replied the Sentinel.

— Thank you for your service, I will do what I can to ward off what is chasing — Prosopher said.

In fact, we don't even know what to do, so Aesus and I decided to get rid of the pedestal so that we could go to the end of the courtyard ourselves.

— Tree, we have things to discuss with you.

— I am here! — replied the Elder Tree.

— We want to get off the pedestal, get rid of the branches that have raised us up. We can't stay here while what's out there gets lost in the chaos.

— Cyrus made up his mind.

— I won't ask for what I gave you. Wise trees don't ask for what they give. Don't look to the side, or to the front, or to what's behind us, look to the sky, the higher the stars are, the brighter they shine. — The tree firmly testifies to this.

Then branches began to lift us above the trees, our vision widened, we could see more than the glowing garden. We observed the manifestation that had accumulated, forests that had lost their glow, backyards that were unhappy even with the sunlight of the day.

We concentrate saying: the higher the stars are, the brighter they shine. The advice of an ancient tree, the fireflies, listening to it, repeated it over and over again. Our lightness increased, and as a result, we reached the top through the branches, feeling that we demanded discharge the energy we had accumulated, we held on until we couldn't take it anymore, shining beyond the limits of the garden. The groves told us that Phagonellas decided to move away, as the light was too strong for them to drain. The glow subsided, and trees lowered us back to the plinth, the vigilantes fanned out outside the yard, remedying the gloom.

"It's only a matter of time before they return. We are too bright." — spoke Aesus alarming him

" I understand your concern, do you still want to get rid of the plinth?" — asked Prosopher.

"As the watch-lamp told us, we are a small part of a big thing. I believe that we should direct ourselves where it will sink" — suggested Aesus.

"Let's take it easy and see what we'll do." — replied Prosopher uncertainly.

It seemed like some enchantment, the flowers bent their stems towards us, for we had shone like a star in the middle of woods, not even the big trunks could protect our light, the trees took more roots below, above and above us, a light shining in the center, between the branches and the roots.

The dream of happy days came true, making up for the nights of sadness, knowing that I am strong for overcoming my own hauntings, even with fear. Today my shine is a transition of my fears, I was afraid to radiate, but I learned from the trees that every broken branch is an incentive to reform itself.

One day, the guards told me they spotted a glow like ours in the distance, but that they were looking for us, I asked about the closer Cyrus, would it be two Sentinels united?

I told them to look for that luminance similar to ours. Until they found him, leading to me.

Two burly auroras "facing" each other…

"I came from Clarendel to give you a message."

— Clarendel? I don't know where you came from. — replied Prosopher, finding it odd.

— Where I was born, you were born. You will have to separate, ceasing to be Foz, to be vigilant. — ordered the light of Clarendel.

— And why should we listen to you? — Aesus answered him.

— If this continues, I will have to separate them by force. There are already too many fireflies here that need to roam. Darkness is strengthening in the groves that are weakest. Where they shine, the trees stop breaking their branches, flowers stop dying, fruits don't fall or rot, rains no longer flood the soil. You have barred yourselves, on the other hand, you have made the gardens that are scarcer of light more vulnerable — spoke the light with propriety.

— We can wander again if you like. So that's what you have faith in? At the end of things? I thought the lights brought hope. — said Prosopher, trying to pacify.

— Our brilliance one day ceases, even hope gives up hope one day. There is no option left, if not, this one. For the end of things to be its beginning. — replied the fire of Clarendel.

An energy similar to a handle came out and undid the rose, its petals fell like tears when they fall from the eyes, when all perished, the little light showed itself. He grabbed Aesus and pulled him from me, and at that moment the light that surrounded me, embodied itself in the form of a firefly, and the same with me, we have the equal amplitude now. The bright went away, among the bushes, its light was fading, similar to the sun at dusk… we were left alone… everything I believed is a doubt now.

— The way we shone one day couldn't tell how much I enjoyed being with you. — declared Aesus.

— Don't say that, we should try to unite again, connect our brightly aerials. — said Prosopher in a sweet tone.

— If we team up, he might come back and tear us apart! For all the pain I'm susceptible to and will feel, I understand that we shouldn't be together. — said Aesus decisively.

Aesus moving away and despair possessing my judgments, the mothers of woodland ignored us for having said that we would swim in the winds again, not even the old tree forgave us. The roots and branches that were stretching towards us, weakened, and I was left only to myself. Floating, sensing myself fallen, like broken branches, crumpled, torn, perforated leaves, I am a leaf that does not support the fall of its own branch, when it detaches itself, It takes them with it.

Never touched the ground, and it still felt like a broken branch. I am a light without hope, a leaf torn apart and taken to the anthill, a branch torn aside by its own feelings. When I could finally imagine that wouldn't be abandoned, I was thrown into the winds and let them take me where they wanted.

Before Aesus walked away completely, I said to him:

— Aesus, he gives direction to the lost, myself are astray, but I will find you, because you are the direction of my path. Remember what the Elder Tree asked you to do. — He declared with intensity.

Where would I go without the path that was with me? Without the advice of those who are wise, how can I shine and not see my way? I am blind?

Have my lights been undone? Where did the voice that motivated me go? Or am I only distressed by shining so brightly? I assume that ignored my destiny living a path that myself created, thought I was the protagonist of my story, but my story was already written, and I have no other vocation, I will fly like a firefly without the fire of hope.

Seeing the darkened trees, I chose one of them, when I got close to its trunk it opened a crack. Just entered, the live woods, when in need of lumi nance, allow the lights to enter.

"Sentinel! Many of you protect yourselves with us, and forget that darkness punishes us when we are light inside." — complained the tree.

— Today I'm weak, I've been through dark places and haven't even been beaten, even though wanted to. I was once told that the hungry are not interested in skinny chandeliers. — said Prosopher, overcome with anguish.

— What are you so sad about, little glow?" His words sound sad. — replied the tree.

— I never suspected that a light could despair, instead of taking hope with it. — said Prosopher, dissatisfied.

— We tree are born from the bottom like a seed, there it is dark, silent, there is nothing but ourselves, nevertheless, nothingness is the food of everything. Some lights weren't born out of the dark, so they don't know what faith in good things means. Only the luckiest understanding that ho ping is better than despairing, we don't need to be encouraged by everything, but we must always encourage ourselves. — counseled.

— Not only the leaves live here, but wisdom makes you an inn. That light told me that we were born from the same cause, yet we are so different. — said Prosopher calmly.

— Look at the vegetation, even though it is full of trees, some only know the darkness of night, they were never seeds that lived their own shadows.— explained the tree.

— Aren't all the scintillation Sentinels?— asked Prosopher out of curiosity.

— It doesn't matter how the lights are born, but how they choose to shine. Little glow, don't hide forever, clarity needs to be seen. — said the tree, instructing him.

I stayed, for many seasons in the tree, the climates had already changed several times, decided to watch, nevertheless, I gave up, got intrigued, I thought, I fought against myself, got confused, and now I don't know where I should go. remembered the gift that the old tree gave, so I fed the wood that shelters me in the evenings, it then grew, blossomed, blossomed, bore fruit, leafed, regrowthed, the branches thickened and branched out, they even touched other trees, the roots deepened, fed other trees.

The trees got bigger, beautiful, they were healed of their pain. I fed them with my glow, I can regenerate my light for some time after using it, and it helped to propagate a varnish in small quantity, without the dark noticing, I built a little grove, in it the trees to me, worshiped in silence. They still gave me the visible radiation, we are reciprocal, we are a hidden sanctuary, what I considered weak led me to fortitude, I, giver of flashes.

The Flesh of the Trees

— There is knowledge about the lightness of those who have wood as a foundation. — said the tree.

— I admit that I don't know the mysteries of the jungle. — said Prosopher.

— When we are illuminated, the light travels in our veins, spreading in structures. Inside the trees live trails that the sparkles can pass. — revealed the tree to Prosopher.

— You suggest I wander with the branches and trunks?— asked Prosopher, not understanding.

— Not just between the branches, but the roots as well. Dim your brightness to get through the narrow passages. Who knows, maybe the answers you're looking for are in the difficult passages? — clarified the Trail Tree.

— Maybe life is an endless journey of darkness that walks to meet, and lights that wander in order to shine. Every bright has a shadow that accompanies it, there is no torch that your flame does not create sombre. — Prosopher expressed his knowledge.

I said goodbye to the sanctuary, diminished me, spreading most of my brilliance in the environment, a glow that was already weak seemed to be off, withal, sparks disappear in the eyes and light up the heart. What I considered insignificant looked enough to me, wanted to shine all the time, and even the sun hides its lighthouse in the bushes of stars. Traveled along, passing by the roots that were connected, some that came out of the ground, others had an end and I had to return by the way I came from, others that were so deep that they nestled in the abyss. I overcame the biggest root, persevered in the descent, reached the depths, the precipice, the abyss.

I realized that one spark is a great light in the waters of depth. Everything given to the little is much, so it happened. A spark that I thought was small, fit into the scarcity of the glow. Likewise, even in the chaos that once inhabited me, I saw a lot of Phagonellas who didn't even know to move, as I didn't. Also saw Sentinels, lights just born, who would be victims of their given fate. Some glowed like Axanar, perhaps to dispel the duskiness, see a glowing veil emanating from an opening at the top, a radiance ball rising from it, one firefly? So I ran quickly towards the curtain, which had already begun to retreat, and managed to catch up with it. Every time it moved away from the Sentinel, the curtain took on its glow, and it turned gray because its halo was taken away. The veil took me, as if it were a transfer, through a short passage, and then, as I left it, I could behold a great glory, impossible to measure, from four points, the sparkle of that Sentinel directed toward the great star, and the more I left the passage, more I realized that my glory was nothing.

Looking at the praise of place I am, just as an allegory that I was just a spark among many stars, is this Clarendel? In it there is a dome proportional to the place, with scintillations that did not look like fireflies as they were very large, each one maneuvered in its functions, at least it looked. They sang very compatible, synchronized, harmonic sounds, they were superior in intelligibility, skill, unity, would it be a better version of lightwatchers?

There are various lounges on the grounds. One of them is dark, as if it were dusk. Mist floated through the room, though it didn't pass through any doors that were closed in the hall. Between rooms is a huge throne with a golden statue that reflects the light of the sun and directs it to a great four-pointed star, I believe it feeds on its brightness, my own light taught me that brightness devours darkness, which didn't make sense, a higher luminosity I saw was powered by the glare and darkness coming from hall, it didn't need balancing.

Some mysteries took place I could not unravel, writings that I was unable to translate, phenomena saw by my "eyes" for the first time, magnitudes beyond my normal range, had to go back to organize so many events in my clarity, felt that I am unprepared, do not understand anything of all that already understood.

My ignorance betrayed me, feeling as if it is too early to look for the answers I wanted, therefore, leading myself to the dome with the intention of getting out of it, before crossed it, noticing that some were entering and passing inside, so I continued, when just about to leave, something covered me, a bubble formed, revealing my identity to them, I heard someone say: "someone there!" And I'm trapped in a golden bubble, and it takes me into a room.

A glow spells out:

— Introduce yourself, fragment of fire. — he told me.

— There's nothing to show. I am nobody before the celestial glory. — Prosopher hid his truths

— I've never seen a sparkle so diminished, my lights couldn't notice. — the fire was impressed.

— What the eyes cannot sense, only the soul can feel. — said Prosopher.

— Nothing goes in and out without permission from the dome. How did you get here? — strange, the fire.

— The sparks of soul go to the impossible places to reach. — declared Prosopher mockingly.

— Hide your truth and you'll remain trapped in a bubble. — said the fire to frighten.

This light has retreated, stealing my freedom, and even in captivity I'm bound to the Sentinel mission, worried about my luminous garden, the hidden sanctuary, would it survive the duskiness? Have a chance to obscurity discover the secret of light in the hidden sanctuary? I remember where the veil brought me from, going to that passage, but what needs to be done now is get out of the bubble. When I touch it, it hardens like a stone, I've tried everywhere and doesn't work. The bubble was luminous, which clarified my judgments: what if I let go of my aglow fragments, turn into a Phagonela and try to escape?

I released all my sparks of radiance, the dust did not pass until I darkened and managed to pass through the orb barrier, when I emerged chaos ensued, my disorder wanted to absorb all the remaining luminosity including this barrier, but I only drained the energy that belonged to me and the bubble stayed there to prevent it from emitting too much, who knew I would have more control over myself, for many times that have I been taken by darkness? Recognizing that I can control my emotions, even when I am deep in my own shadows

Passing through a lower crack of a door in the hall, I looked at the center, in that area where the throne and statue were, magnificent, golden, an unusual beauty, It also appeared that there was a coupled force, difficult to explain the grandeur of this humanoid monument. As I floated in a golden courtyard, waiting for the opening to dissolve so that the veil would take me in same way it brought me, after some time they noticed my absence, then a few sparkling orbs emitted a distorted clarity on a surface trying to find me, of wandering and floating, escaped them all and managed to enter the passage. Mantle took us, and as I looked at the seeds a little higher from where I stood, seeing the stems when they were immature. With me was a light, probably just born, a Sentinel, and we were left in the abyss. The exact time that veil charged its light, I drank it, and the veil withdrew, and I gave the brightness to negligent, turning him into a lightwatcher.

— I have to thank you a lot, I don't remember where I came from, who I am and why I'm here. Slight moments of anguish hurt enough. — said the sentinel.

— I was born like you, the same pain you felt, I felt. You won't know what you came for, and I'm not your guide, since I don't even know how I should guide myself. Other lights will come to give you a mission, but take your walk and make it your mission. — Prosopher advised him.

— Everything is still too much for me, feeling like the death of a star and the birth of a new one, is weird, I don't understand myself. Could I follow you? — he asked Prosopher.

— What would you follow me for?— Prosopher asked him.

— It's easier for two to find each other than one.— he said.

— Your words remind me of someone. I name you Haddon, who is found to be lost. If you want to follow me, follow me and even if I don't know about everything, I know one thing: don't stop lighting up, do good. — declared Prosopher.

The memories of Aesus came to me through an innocent's light, remembering moments of my happiness without being alone, if it hurt, it hurt for two, pleasure was as vivid as my memories, good times that unfolded. Only the winds know where "my way" is, but their blows insist on keeping this secret.

I went to exit of the abyss on shiny roads, little by little it makes the exit that takes us to the woods, when I arrived there, I saw traces of luminous dust floating in air, so we followed it, taught Haddon to cross trunks and "walk" through the branches, we traveled to luminous garden, Haddon was hypnotized by the fluorescent flowers and glowing leaves, he had just seen the most beautiful garden, who would not be enchanted by such grace? A rhyme of the garden through poetry of the lights, the song of sparkles, the trees, petals that illuminate in sadness, a garden that fades during the day and lights up at dusk, who would not be enchanted by poems written with the soul of someone who shines?

— What seat does the luminiferous dust come from? — asked Prosopher curiously.

— Although we grieved for you, we bleed in small particles for your lack, so we prayed that our shards would reach you, the garden needs light when it gets dark. — said the Elder Tree of the forest of light.

— While I was away, I built a shrine, and my radiance will take care of you as if you were me. — said Prosopher.

— May one day be me, connected to a backyard of wonders. — said Haddon, impressed.

— Your light is so great, I'm very surprised to be so diminished. — said the Elder Tree upon noticing him.

— Too big sparkles don't get into narrow passages, — replied Prosopher.

— A very humble lesson. — said the tree, appreciating his wisdom.

— I will always travel between my sanctuaries. — said Prosopher.

I went back to the secret orchard, where one day a tree said to me, "sometimes it's better if our torch burns only for us". When I heard these short words the brightness itself sobered me, for too much brilliancy is a fever, and I had many fevers of brilliance for the fanaticism of my dawn.

Be bright is be a survivor of life's disturbances, to reflect light even when it is dark, duskiness does not define who we are, but we define who we are by what we do with our own duskiness. When we arrived at the secret orchard, I could see the obscurities and not only what appears to our eyes, withered leaves, trees with dry branches, aged trunks, injured woods.

— Haddon, Hide in a tree trunk, the Algozes are loose. — Prosopher warned.

Then the invaders appeared, in their most powerful forms, they were many Algozes, shadows formed from other shadows, which made them more hungry for light. I dimmed my fire even more with intent to make them unaware of my presence and escaped to a higher point of a hidden sanctuary, to the top of a tree where I took shelter, while they tried to cross over the trunk where Haddon was hiding. But woods are lovers of lights, only we can pass through their doors.

The Algozes cannot perceive the presence of a spark, but leaves can, So I entered, following tracks to the hollowest part.

— My inn, trail tree, help me restore our orchard. — asked Prosopher.

— Prosopher, he who gives light, go to my roots and lighten, my flesh is his, his light is mine. — said the Tree of Paths.

I encouraged myself, went to the roots near Algozes and concentrated my dim light. The tree where Haddon is hiding asks for help, though I do not want it to suffer, it was necessary to save us.

The candle grew stronger, brightness piercing the earth above the roots, a hope coming from below, which is not a tree habit, they look to the stars that illuminate them. I began to open the clay and illuminated roots climbed me, and his tormentors moved away, the tree Haddon stayed in, allowed him to leave, and he prepared himself for the tormentors, turning them into Sentinels, I directed my energy at him, with intent not to grant your Phagonela perversion. The roots of other live woods tore through soil and reached me as soon as the Algozes left, just like some

Phagonellas became fireflies. I let what was left of my light in the sanctuary shine out beyond it in small shining particles, and whatever it reached finally healed. I now live for the flesh of trees, so I made a shining path, protected by Sentinels, and placed Haddon to guides lighting guards. Not only that, but I grouped the Fozes in those most vulnerable places, there are cracks for the Phagonellas to enter. This path connects our Hidden Orchard and the Luminescent Garden, which I call Home of the Fireflies, Luminescent Sanctuary. Voices of guardians, like flutes, echoing in gardens, in woods, inviting other lights, the more that arrive, the more they disperse in darkness of woods, to turn Algozes into Fozes, Phagonellas into guardians, benevolence must anesthetize violence

I swam among the waves of winds and the breaths in words called me, it was the Old Tree of Luminous Garden, I rushed toward it.

"Everything you've built is a marvel, I never assumed that dazzles were born when the order of things was disrupted." said the Old Tree.

— I didn't break the ordinances, I broke with my ignorance. — explained Prosopher.

— Many times our ignorance is our cages, living in cycles that imprison us like chains. — explained the Elder.

— New paths, new lives. I saw Clarendel's rule by the roots, they control everything the way they want. — said Prosopher to the tree.

— Do you want to break their law? — asked the Elder, as if it were something hideous.

— Burn for your regime to be undone. — said Prosopher intensely.

— Have you got something planned yet? — the Elder asked him.

— Not yet, and I don't even know how to start.—said Prosopher.

— There's something about us that fireflies don't know. And that can change everything. — explained the Elder tree.

— What do you plan? — asked Prosopher.

— Not every wood is just a wood, some of them contain a sleeping human being. These are the talking trees, they live between being flesh and wood. — explained the elder.

— I traveled in a wood speaker's veins and missed any traces of humanity.— disbelieved Prosopher.

— The body is with the wood, because the body is the wood and the wood is a tree. — explained the Elder.

— How would that help? — asked Prosopher.

— A human tree is capable of many things, but it is limited by its flesh and wood. There is the right moment to be a human and a tree, but when I am a human, the tree remains in me, when I am a tree, the human side sleeps. We call the humanoid a walker because of the abandonment of the roots, having to make an effort with the legs to walk, even though the legs stop one day to create other roots. — Explained in detail to Prosopher, Elder Tree.

— So, if you are in the form of wood, do you wish to carnify yourself? — asked Prosopher.

—Yes. A condition prevents me from transforming myself: the blossoms are natural and the flesh too, like wood, to transform myself I need the changes flow, I must not prevent them, otherwise I will suffer and there is no way I can force my human metamorphosis. Even so, during the moments that you shone, I felt my heart wanting to be alive. — explained the tree.

— So my scintillation will change you? — asked Prosopher.

— Perhaps your light will free me from the wooden cages? — instigated the possibility.

— And what way do you keep that secret from lightwatchers? — Prosopher suspected.

— The human, at birth, emerges from the clay. Throughout life, we deposit our heart in the earth, feeding it with our roots, until the body is fully structured. — explained the Elder.

— Trees live in the midst of very delicate processes. — commented Prosopher.

— But that doesn't matter now, come to me, we'll see if I can turn human by your bright. — said the Elder.

The trunk made a small crack, I passed through it, as I entered into its hollow center, wooden veins that were thicker approached me. I stayed for a while, carrying my light until it was quite bright, then I released it in small fractions, the tree began to fluoresce, its flowers fell, and new trees grew around it, fruits sprouted and fell. Eventually leaves did not resist, turning orange from the excess of light, but they gave up to stay on the branches.

 "It's time they found out who the talking trees are." said the Elder Tree to the shrine.

The main branches of Old Tree fell apart, stretching out into arms, it had some leaves on it, its trunk broke into a few pieces, revealing the tree-human, and I like a halo over her head. It is taller than ordinary humans, hair has greenish tones, and although made of flesh, the structures still resemble the wood.

 "Wood suffers like flesh, like Sentinels in darkness." clarified the Elder of the flora.

"We are so different, yet so similar. Starting today, we will be the protectors of the Luminescent Shrine." declared Prosopher to her and to all of them.

The Elder Tree put its arms in the mud, forming multiple stems that encircled the entire temple from outside, only lightwatchers would be able to pass because these stems emit short flashes that keep the phagocytes away from the forest.

— One light shines in many and even by itself, but the flashes drive away those who would devour it.   — said the Elder.

— Before, I believed the shadows would be my enemy, but I was wrong, the light intimidates me. Clarendel needs to be stopped — said Prosopher with determination.

The Lightwatcher Mission

I am a light that turned on in the dark, I lived in a deep abyss, I am not a seed, but My brightness emerged and grew independent, however, that same light shows me the way for those in darkness, be it a tree man, a lightwatcher, roses and all kinds of gardens of the humanities in question, every garden needs clarity to be beautiful, and in the same form of obscurity, Sentinels like me, it brightens the flowers when it becomes night, the dawn of dusk, the glow that emanates from the flora, light known by the living of the dark, photon that makes trees grow, walkers bloom and make them rose like lamps.

"Sentinels, similar to me, are a luminosity in a vast fog at dusk, no matter how the night could be opaque, dark, smoky, dazzling, they cannot fail to be seen, Sentinel is to be a difference where everyone acts as equals, it is to shine light even with the darkness, there are those who shine through the shadows, this one is filled with himself and his ego, still manages to deceive by a false clarity. Sentinels are fluorescent mosses in a forest, we are conspicuous for our good qualities."

I said all these words to Eldest, giving a complete judgment to the fireflies that follow me and take shelter in the tabernacle as well as beyond it. The Elder Tree conjured from her hands a trunk with straight thorns, which she called the Scroll of Luminous Wood.

Many charms the tree-human is competitive as far as I can see, so I wonder what the Trail's Tree would do at meeting the Elder, a meeting of sage speakers I have ever judged.

— We could go to the Trail Tree, maybe she is the way we're going to confront Clarendel. — suggested Prosopher to Eldest.

— It would be important to know the paths of her trails. — said the Elder.

We went, appreciating the wonders of the woods and the glowing wanderers, we were in a world of dwarf sparkles, of radiant dust, of glossy branches.

We cross the luminous path.

Furthermore, we neared it, the tree now is huge, flowering, blooming from roots to branches in the hidden tabernacle.

— I'm looking for a space in you that's free of flowers and I can't find it, I'm impressed — said Prosopher admiringly.

— I have transcended the blossoms themselves, thanks to the harmony of the sanctuary and its connection with luminous garden. I notice you have changed from a firefly to a halo, with tree-human at the bottom. Remarkable his knowledge now, of what the trees do not speak, though they are chatty. — replied the Tree of Paths (same of Trail Tree).

— This is the Elder Tree in my garden, it is currently in its human phase, my brightness has accelerated its humanity. It revealed the secret that you hid for a long time. — said Prosopher.

— Amazing what lights can do. We must not rush our development, we must allow it to flow naturally. — advised the Tree of Paths

— We risked ourselves for a greater cause. I discovered the lights that subjugated me, destroyed the union between me and Aesus. — said Prosopher with conviction.

— Will you risk retaliation? — asked the Tree of the Paths.

— I do not intend revenge. But in undoing the order of things they created, I visited the abyss and closely witnessed them transforming the Sentinels into Phagonellas. I felt compassion for them, they will be condemned for the missions they will give. — declares Prosopher in a passive tone.

— You, who knows the ways, what courses shall we take to stop them? — asked the Elder, from tree to tree.

— In life, not only good things last, but some bad things are necessary. Take care of the trees, they allow storms and flagitious come to them. Take the shortcut you think is best, but remember the consequences of it. Teachings I learned living, which led me to write the scroll called: The Path and the Walker. — said the Tree of the Paths to them.

We were silent for a while, we revered the wood of the trails and when we were about to leave, a noise sounded from its trunk, the tree stretched out becoming convex towards us, thick at its base and thin at the end, it cocked all the corners, branches into one. At the tip were many closed petals, we touched them, which perpetrated their opening, exposing the largest seed I had ever seen.

"Eat the seed. Elder." said the Tree of Paths mysteriously.

She ate, and the transformations sprouted in her limbs, branches were born encircling her arms and legs, on her heels there were tiny roots, her neck was covered by two leaves, as if she had the tree and the human aligned inside her.

"Use this gift when it is necessary, you are now a human and a tree, the seed shows the power of growth." instructed the Tree of Paths.

From the advice given by the Tree of the Trails, I remember her saying: look for the lost parchment, The Path and the Walker, there is written the answers that you really will face in life. These words are stuck in me. How would I find something that I don't know where it is? Foliage on the roads which did not reveal the path I should take, he instructed me to look for the path without saying who he was and where I could follow him with my lamps.

In the region I left Haddon, at the entrance to the hidden shrine, lamps accosted in the woods of Luminous Sanctuary.

"Haddon, I see three watchers pulling up!" warned the guard.

—From what I've been instructed by Prosopher, they're not lightwatchers. — said Haddon.

— Clarendel lamps? — asked Foz.

— I've never seen a lamp with a luminous ring in the middle or protected by shiny shells.— They probably are. Haddon explained.

— Let us pass, we want to speak with Prosopher. — protested the lights.

— Of course! — answered Haddon, but not wanting them to enter.

After they passed and became distant...

— What are you doing? Was it my position in the parts susceptible to attacks? — answered Foz about Haddon's attitude.

— I don't know their abilities, and since we're experts in dealing with darkness, is there a way to fight light with light? — said Haddon, and the twinkles reflected.

The song changed, there were loud desperate cicadas and the fireflies spread out, opening a passage, in it came three lamps similar to the one in Clarendel. One of them was simple like me, although it was bigger, the other one had a shell that covered a third half of itself, and lastly, the one that with rings moving around, in turns, in total there were two rings, what surprised me the most.

Anything you do could bother, a little breach and they show up. Do we fight or surrender? Causing disorder to create one's own order, shattering the foundations that were imposed on us, begging for life to make us winners of the war of convictions. We are right? Wrong? Of all wisdom learned and instructed me, I am still a layman with all that has happened.

The twinkle that surprised me the most speaks to me:

"May Thallasus' brilliance convert you, Prosopher." Clarendel lamps.

— I refuse to be blessed by her. When I was Cyrus of the Forest, they removed me from that position, and you are responsible. — countered Prosopher showing his indignation with the elite.

— You want a power you can't contain. — Clarendel lamps.

— You misunderstand me. I wish that fireflies are freed from their norms, if possible they can be happy as they are. — justified Prosopher.

— Would you sacrifice everything for this? There are many things you don't know and shouldn't know, especially about human trees.— answered Claren's lamp.

— Lamps that keep knowledge between them. They never shared their radiance, they would never be aware of what it is to be a candle. — said Prosopher, stating his opinion of the Clarens.

— The Cyrus, they are the same as the Fozes, living in the woodlands, even if they are rare. But you, we couldn't let, you took on a greater proportion than we imagined. — explained the lamp of Clarendel his knowledge.

— Let the truth be perpetuated, Clarendel fears my power. — said Prosopher arrogantly.

— Great powers call for cautious measures. Apparently you don't know what you are, not a Sentinel, there were others just like you, however, no one has ascended in so many centuries in this way, considering the memory of his birth has been erased. — uttered the flame of Clarendel in order to sum up Prosopher's ignorance.

— What am I by any chance?— asks Prosopher.

— All we've said are the words you need to know. You have five days, get rid of this place! — replied Clarendel's lamp as if Prosopher were not worthy of answers.

The light of rings made them grow, the other two grew closer, splitting the earth and forming a rupture, until the luminous rings diminished, a short flash was formed and when it dissipated, they disappeared.

— Elder Walker, I think that is supposed to warn! — said Prosopher.

— What is natural can be hurt, but the trust in time heals it, Prosopher. — counselled the Elder Walker quietly.

— It reminded me about the Tree of Trails, which even decided to shut up. — said Prosopher.

The wanderer of the foliage, walker-tree or human-tree, as it is called in the tabernacle, covered the rupture by conjuring up woods that crossed each other, so that animals, humans or plants would not grow inside it or fall into it, proving that wounds can be healed, Regardless of the hole it has made in our being, it is necessary to understand that heal is the time.

"We have five sunsets. That aren't enough to find the Trail Tree scroll, so we'll focus on protecting the garden."

Prosopher announced to the garden's immigrants and its residents.

— I wanted to intensify my twinkle. The way they are, I don't have enough hours to match them. — exclaimed Prosopher to Elder Walker.

— Gratitude for the chance! We still have some time. What if you drain the energy of a few wards?— asked the Walker.

— It would be insufficient. I will abandon the justification of light and let chaos rule me. — said Prosopher confidently.

— If that's what you're going to do, make it work.— replied the Walker.

I summoned all who watch and said:

"To all who watch in the most beautiful garden, Clarendel confronts us. Stay in the confines of our sparkling garden, defending it, the candles, stay close to the Ancient Walker and me. As great as the evil is, we can overthrow them with the whiteness of our goodness." announced Prosopher.

On the first day, I didn't worry so much about what might happen. The fallen leaves reminded me of the seed, and I don't know the place that favors its growth. The tree of the trails bent down, joined its branches as if they were one, since then it was silent.

A fraction of my halo changed into a shining form, I saw Aesus, Axanar, Phagonellas that I saved, saw when I was like a star, so tall and flowery, remembered the voice I heard, but today it is silent, heard from many sages that silence is an answer, which I disbelieve. The signs of life warn us because they speak, rather than being mute.

It's been terrible the bright vision of reality, like see the life without your clothes, at one point, I felt certain that of living in an exquisite world, I got used to the peace of mind of the luminous gardens, forgetting everything in Clarendel, and of all the agony I've lived. Although my body is an orbit, my mind is a sparkle, my voice is poetry, I have feelings, regardless of not being flesh my structures, I suffer just like anyone who has. Tried to escape from the past in a few daydreams, as I dragged it with me, today, before sunset, I will hold reality in my hands, hands that I don't have, since it is not matter, but the poetry of my radiance will take me where I have to go.

On the second day, I made peace with all possible foliage, being kind and attentive to the trees, provided what they needed, and they allowed me to penetrate their structures. I swam on the trails of all the trees, floated on several hollow trunks, even if I tried to force them to develop, their hearts are too asleep in the woods. I got to know the roots, many of them, those so grandiose, that extend into the darkest parts.

On the third day, regarding the beings of the natural sanctuary, I understood that victory depended on more than just the Sentinels, but on the garden's will to prevail, it was beyond my own motivations, our harmony will make us win, we need to be one.

"The luminescent garden is a tree with many branches, take the example of the wisest tree in the hidden shrine, it united its body in one. My victory is yours, your will is mine, I am the head and you are my body, we need each other." said Prosopher on the fourth day. Message I asked the human-tree to attach to the luminiferous parchment.

Fifth and final day... the song of the fireflies grew sad, the sparkling leaves withdrew to the trees, earth became dry, flowers repressed their petals, the plants tried to hide where they were born, the garden desperate because of the light and not the shadows. The mission given to me had already been annihilated, before I took care of perverts across the abyss, currently, I prefer to learn from the profound than what is superficial to the eyes. I could see beyond idealizations, blinded by imprisoned convictions, enlightenment can corrupt as much as darkness.

I walked to the highest point of garden, delivering a message to them:

"I know you are apprehensive, afflicted, afraid, but fear is the strength of those who shine, they took away your hope, so did mine, nevertheless, you are my hope, once some wise tree said to me: we don't need to be encouraged by everything, but always encourage ourselves. And if you can't, I'll do it." encouraged Prosopher the luminescent shrine.

I took the luminiferous parchment and read some messages the Elder Walker had written.

Words that made courage live with us, I encouraged them, although I needed to do it for myself first. I heard the tides call my name, they invited me to be the rock in the middle of the sea, no matter if wave crashes it won't knock it over. We are strong even with downcast sparkles, because the union of those who weaken makes them stronger, fear is our fuel to shine.

The trees surrendered, their branches expanded, their leaves opened, the roots became more exposed, the flowers decided to show their beauty to what confronted them, fear. The plants stopped bending towards the ground and leaned towards me, each in their own way of saying, I'm with you, but the Tree of Trails remained mute and inert.

It was evening and they each went to their positions, the Fozes stayed on our side, the Sentinels headed towards the ends of the garden. At dusk, we wait for the birdsong to tell us the midnight moment, we were already distracted when they appeared, not even the birds managed to sing. Rifts in the heavens opened, Clarendel, lights showed in a mighty way, hundreds of them.

I will pursue my purpose with the garden.

My mission is to preserve the good from the evils that pretend to be like it. I'm Sentinel, no matter what they think I am.

War of Convictions

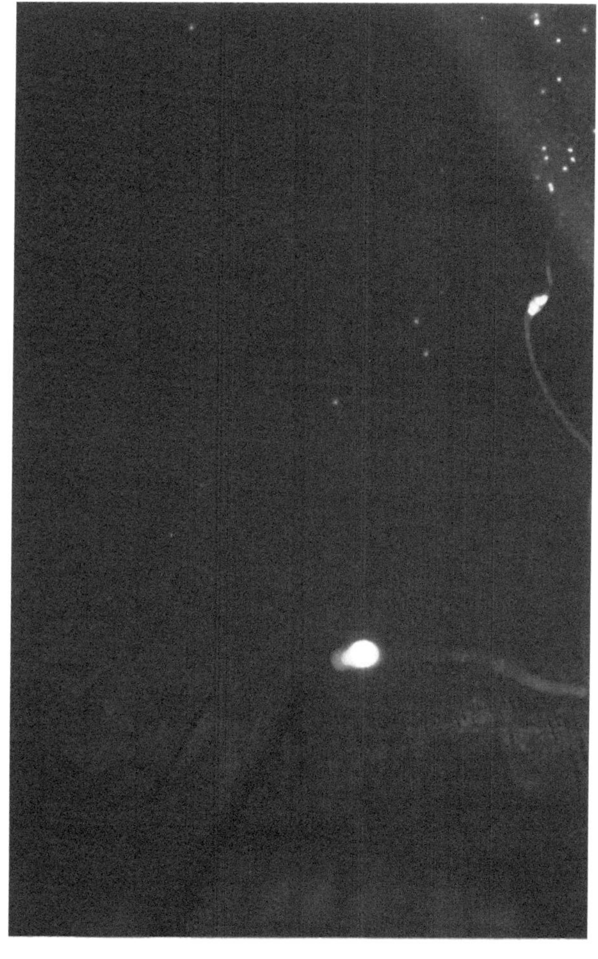

I changed as they charged, from a halo to a spark, it will be difficult to find me, for the reason that I am a light in the flesh of trees. They pressed our Sentinels with glare around the woodland, causing our retreat, they directed their energy to form cavities, like one I was trapped in, and some of us were weakened.

The Elder Walker put up wooden walls on the path connecting the two parts of the sanctuary, but they go across, punishing the woods with light, impossible to stop them, at that moment I understood the lamps healed and also condemned.

During the fall of woods, the Cyrus were concentrated, creating a huge flash, but when they ran out, those who had a shield locked them in the bag.

"What trunk is Prosopher hiding in? Say!" said the Clarendel lamps authoritatively.

— Explain to me the reason for ending up with a happy garden, and I'll tell you. — challenged them, the Elder Walker.

— Tree human, you have a conscience yourself. The existence of everything depends on greater control over the order of things. — said Clarendel's squire.

— Life is a constant transformation, some things should not remain as they are. — said the Elder, stalling for time.

— You're right. How about being transformed? — said Clarendel's squire.

It threw a lightning bolt into the human tree, knocking her to her knees and paralyzing her.

— That's enough! — shouts Prosopher.

My voice echoed like a scream that hurt those who had no ears, the twinkle listens to what the sparkles speak, that is, everything, because every thing that is alive has bright in your veins.

And the one who lives like being, but is not alive, does he have light?

An enormous flash opened the ground, pushing them away by the luminous force, my light floated close to them when leaving the crater, I walked inside the roots in the form of a Phagonela, wearing luminance that was mine, absorbing their bright, they could not sniff out who perverted him, didn't know how to act.

The bags fell apart, the watchers offered their brightness to me, while absorbing fractions of the obscurity, so that it would not be corrupted, the darkness came from me, including. I needed help, help to make the shimmer and shadow. The Elder gave me the rest of the light that her heart necessitated, and other Sentinels joined in, donating light and absorbing duskiness, the ones that are now loose. Brightness and chaos coming at me simultaneously, surrounding me and I sucking in. By virtue of having so much power, I was raised in the garden; the more I assumed them, the more heaven wanted me as one of its stars.

Their configuration was changing, so I forged a halo that trapped one, I will question him about who I am.

My bright turned greenish, at which point the luminance and shadows aligned, I descended slowly, making a wish to the luminiferous dust itself.

"Restore the wounded, keep intact, regenerate the skeletons in the garden." he uttered in whispers.

"Call me Prosopher, the Emerald of the Garden, the wise tree's blessing to the world." he declared to everyone present.

Clarendel's lights didn't become Phagonellas due to lack of light, they petrified in a circular shape, and only I managed to stop them, maybe I'm not a Sentinel like they said.

Everyone who witnessed it wasn't happy, they saw me in a cruel image, by the solidification of the Clarens. Everything I asked to restore was repaired, but not the Elder, nor the Tree of the Paths, and the lamps of Clarendel. The Elder froze, the Tree of the Trails continued on its course, and Claren's were like stones with perfect circumference.

— I did not allow petrification to take him. — Prosopher began a dialogue.

— Why didn't you leave? — ask Clarendel's lamp.

— I need to know who I am. — said Prosopher, expecting the light of Claren to give him an answer.

— I won't tell you, for all you've done. — said Clarendel's lamp.

— My deeds are good for me and for those who follow me, in your view yours too. We just see the world from different perspectives, because we lived in an unequal past. — told Prosopher.

— I will. I'm not convinced, but I can tell to kill your ignorance. — It vindicated his words, the fire of Clarendel.

— Of what am I a layman? — asked Prosopher, wanting to understand.

— All lights are daughters of Thallasus, and she is the progeny of the sun, the main star of the world, she has four points and in two of them a kind of light is born. There are four types of brights, the stars, Thallasus and the Sun, Purines who are pure brightness without the darkness, those who dwell in Clarendel, the Sentinels, are light-dark, and finally the Morphous, sparks that shape themselves, can change the size of their sparklife, to associate in the material, even the color is possible to be changed, and they can learn skills from others. Thallasus tries not to generate Morphous, as they are a problem in the society of lights, destabilizing the glows they can. Not yet there is a way to avoid them, as they are born at the same point as Sentinels, which is on the left, Purines on the right. Thallasus receives light at the top, and darkness at the bottom, transferring it into his creations. — he explained as best he could to Prosopher.

— Their congregational support cries out for revolution. I want to go to the glory of stars, wander between the depths of the sea and the heights of the earth, I will be what I want to be, I will never see myself the way you defined me. — Prosopher empowered himself.

— His words write megalomania in the very essence, and his ruthlessness is rooted in a grandiose vision of himself. — he criticized Prosopher with words.

— Before tearing me apart with your declarations, explain to me what is essence and nasty. — asked Prosopher once more.

— The essence of light is to shine, it can be lost on the journey, but if we are persevering in it, we will find it again. The acuity is our being that lodges in the depths of our sparkle, determining the difference between us, a purine loses its acuity when its radiance fades, and we never go back, on the watchers, its acuity is undone when taking away its light and its darkness at the same time, and the morphous too, only the purines and the stars are pure in light. Sentinels are born as Phagonellas until they are helped, a morphous is the only one that is reborn from the darkness itself, without needing help, just equalizing its aspects. For each type of luminous being, a type of sharpness, defining the affinities we will have.—described the naturalness of the lights to Prosopher.

— Conceptions my enlightenment is incapable of absorbing. — replied Prosopher, feigning incomprehension.

— Your luminary has no profession, the conception you must understand is your morphosis. There is no place for you in the society of lights. — said the lamp.

— I prefer to become stone than this culture of Thallasus, look at all I've built, why would I need Clarendel? I am the fire that shelters in the flesh of trees, the trunk is my home, my home is what welcomes me and not where I came from. — said Prosopher confidently.

I cast all my light on the immediate surroundings, becoming Phagonela, taking its spark, and its features petrified. Your spark and mine enter again.

— Prosopher, didn't you think it was too much as you took it with the Clarens? — asked some lightwatcher.

— Candles, Flowers, Trees, Fireflies, if we don't fight for what we conquer, they will conquer us. I find their compassion fascinating, but empathy deceives us when we do not know how to handle it, favoring what opposes us. — he said, advising them.

I turned to the tree-human, and no longer seemed so human, the trunk taking form, creating its own shapes, the branches sprouting and the human silhouette disappearing, inert like the Tree of Trails. I shone, I led the spark in her, still, got no response, perhaps she tried to speak, but is she incapacitated, did the blow they dealt her run aground or for the reason I left her to fight? Did she go back to being a tree due to lack of light?

I shared my luminance with the garden, the result of which reduced me to a spark again, I remembered what told me: the trees have trails that allow the passage of sparkles, what if I entered the human-tree? What would you find?

I went in, since the lips were open, I got to know the conformations responsible for human speech, traveled through the heavens after the mouth, every detail was impressionable, interconnected, always leading somewhere. I stopped… in front of a wall and a dark cliff. Likewise, threw myself, falling into a big space, the cliff made me find the seed, which was given by the Tree of Trails. I came here, in fact, in an attempt to wake up the tree, nevertheless, I no longer feel its heart, its warmth and even less its liveliness, there are only woods in place of the body, even though I can see the human structures.

If I shine for the seed, does it come to life?

I concentrated for a while, adjusting my brightness, shining in a reduced portion, apparently nothing happened, then I shined again, in a bigger dose, nothing happened, glowed almost half of it and the seed was luminous, all the same, that's all. I searched for hours a way to exit, at the bottom there was a fissure, nonetheless, I left curiosity aside to return from where I leave alone, without knowing how.

Suddenly, a tree is born, growing quickly, the light has its magic to bring hope in the midst of shadows. The wood that was growing carried me away from the Elder, when I looked saw that it was a large branch, it had some branches on it, but something caught my attention, a leaf at the end of the main branch, it was one, unique, radiant and yellowish, I did not match with one of these so far.

I got close, it unfastened itself in the form of luminiferous dust, its particles came together, a spherical light was generated some rained sparks, echoing a message: I, the Tree of the Trails, died on the verge of taking you to the parchment, don't question it, understand that it was exceptional. If I became human, I would still not know how to direct you, where the scripture is unpronounceable to those who have roots, inaccessible to those who have legs, that's why I associated my twinkle in a seed, reaching the leaves and without them, I'm dead, already that they give me the light I need. Slowly my logs will dismantle, we don't have time, so save your lamentations for now. In the end, my intuition was certain that you would find this message. Follow me!

The bright moved, and I followed it, trying to stay calm, my spark wanting to go out as I tried to shine, dazed by the discontent that came with me.

We went beyond the sanctuary, lands I've never roamed, forest less dense, more open. Pain debilitating from moving, wanted to stop, hide in the logs.

"Go on, Emerald of the Garden." said the fire of the trails.

— The pain I feel is greater than me. — whispered Prosopher, barely speaking.

— It's difficult, lights feel pain even without the flesh, because their souls are wounded. If I pronounce too much or give you a twinkle, I will stop, you won't know what to look for. — said the fire from the trails, consoling him.

— Forgive me. — said Prosopher suddenly,

I took hold of it, its sparkle flowed to me easily, the sparks enveloped me, transmuting me into a clarity that rained glittering particles, my emerald color maintained. At that moment I could hear her in me, comforting my pain, hoping to continue. The chaos reckless had drawn close, but they could only feed on the particles, my glare was too strong for them, so I made them into lightwatchers and they followed me.

A part of the Tree of the Trails now lives in me, like an intuition, while the regeneration I was given merges with it. Both guided me in a part of the forest that did not grow, it only had a few flowers and grass, there were no trees or plants, similar to when I was empty. A voice told me: illuminate! I forced a small flash and a few sparks scattered, revealing the tree hidden by the lights.

— I am the invisible tree, hidden from the eyes and unpronounceable by words, what I keep cannot be accessed. Go back! — warned the Invisible Tree.

— The trail of love brought me here, the wandering tree, the expert in the ways of the spirit. Her glow emanates from me, let me through. — said Prosopher carefully.

— I recognized that you carried her, since you knew how to find me, but I needed to be sure. Only with the soul do we touch another, I feel the Walker of the Trails inside you. She's gone. — said in a slightly sad tone.

— Yes, she sacrificed herself, preferred to abandon her physical body, for a greater cause. — Expressed wanting to resign himself to the situation.

— Trees don't die, they are reborn. I will honor it! — said the hidden tree.

Writings cascade into various sentences across the wood, the scrolls are embedded in the invisible tree.

— Weird. The scripture is a forbidden wooden to be read. — Prosopher was astonished.

— She wrote traditionally, nevertheless, she needed to keep it in someone she trusted. I am forbidden to those who only see what is physical, living within their own limitations.

— How did you become hidden? — asked Prosopher.

— My matter is gone, it will be recycled in other physical constitutions. My spirit is preserved, for this reason I cannot be seen, I am non-existent in what is palpable, a spirit, similar to lights, immaterial. — explained the Invisible Tree.

Every dawn and dusk I discover my lack of knowledge, about myself and what is around me.

On the branches I read:

'we are masterpiece,

tree men with the walker
asleep inside our
trunks, feeding it until
he may awaken.'

That wisdom consoled me, I know that it will not awaken again and will continue in me, through its fire, that's all that is alive in it, in the trails, in the tree, and that its woods will not come back to life.

I said to Trail in myself: thank you for the echoes of you, bringing me this far. Fall asleep scholar of the trails, your paths reached love, rest in the serenity of your soul, too bad you won't wake up anymore.

I read writings contained in the spiritual branches, satiated, as if I didn't need anything, not even light, but understanding life. I had many misunderstandings at the beginning, although I thought I had resolved them, some rested, regarding who I am and why I came into the world. Likewise, I am a star that had just been born, barely knowing how to shine, in addition to representing security in the presence of the tabernacle, since I am insecure, hypocritical with myself for giving purposes, not recognizing mine, the mask which I wore to the attendance of those who follow me, I'm afraid it would fall, my sincere self hid in the back of the stage that I created, the spectacle of light lost in its own brightness. Understanding is the light that guides the darkness of being, realizing yourself is being a Sentinel of your own inconsistencies. I found myself and lost myself, by creating in a moment convictions that were not what I needed, that's why I became disoriented, even though it was light, the illumination radiating in what was postulated, but the essence was evaporated in the skies of the statements that I made. Told to myself, trying to be someone for someone, while distancing myself from what I am.

Thanks to my soul I have seen, that the eyes cannot, in my case, the lights, the conscience taking off the clothes of reality that retires in me, floated on unreal catwalks, walked without legs in an altered perception. I believed that the war of convictions was with others and, in fact, it was with me, the Scroll of the Path and the Walker made me understand that there is no correct path, but there are roads that make us evolve until we touch the stars.

I returned to my garden.

Furthermore, I saw that the tree was more wood than human and the branch that had made me leave it had broken, the Tree of the Trails was already dead, its trunk was dry, aged by the scars, the branches had fallen, most of them, however, she prepared me and her scriptures comforted me. It still hurts a little, about everything.

I rose from the sanctuary, reaching the highest region.

— I surprised everyone, I was what you required with myself needing too, I cared more about others than myself, and in a flash of lights, I focused on my purpose, forgetting what you wanted, peace, and I brought war. The Tree of Trails, which today is faint, taught me that our greatest shadow is what we are. You can allow yourself to shine or be overshadowed by the negativities, many times I had to break my light to be darkness for you, forgetting that the biggest sacrifice had to be for me. — he announced to those sheltered in the sanctuary.

— Take care of the Luminescent Shrine. — said Prosopher.

— What do you intend to do?— asked Haddon in an attempt to comprehension the situation.

— Ending the war I shouldn't have started. — replies Prosopher decisively.

— Perhaps, before revolutionizing the world, we have to revolutionize our being first. I learned from you. — Haddon said respectfully.

— Carry that knowledge with you." If I don't return, you will be the light that guides this place.— said Prosopher, honoring him.

— It is a very high position for someone who was just born. — Haddon showed his modesty.

— Cargo says nothing about us, but what we will be with him. — He made it clear to Prosopher that he had the necessary knowledge, he just lacked experience.

He kept silent and I withdrew.

The Horde of Darkness

I tried to reduce myself to sparks, but I am incapable, my sparkle is too radiant for that, so I decided to go to the city of Clarendel, without the roots. As I am not aware of the path through the earth, I will follow through the atmosphere that is positioned above me.
From the top I can see the place that shines brightest, Clarendel.

The Lightwatchers outside my garden, approached as they were illuminated, questioning among themselves who I am, and I said to them:

"I am Prosopher, giver of flashes, the virtue of regeneration, the heart of tree roots, predecessor of the Luminescent Garden, veneer of the Hidden Sanctuary. My place is on that side, follow the trail of bright mist, it will take you to seats that are your homes." — Reported to those who stayed relatively close.

My mist of light traced the trail to the branches and foliage, leading to the Luminescent Shrine, all leading to the emerald mist, except for two shimmers. One of them is bright and strong, attractive to those who hide in the duskiness, another is weak, almost undesirable for the shadows.

— I know them. Axanar and Aesus. — Prosopher identified them.

— I contemplate the wonders that you have become, I see that you are not a Sentinel. I figured that was. — Axanar said.

— You didn't even know me. I thank you for helping me triumph over my conditions. — said Prosopher.

— Who are you if not a Sentinel? — asked Aesus.

— They called me the morphous, the one who molds himself, even from the dark. But I am released from the definitions that society of light gave me, I am what I am, I am the splendor of those who fail, a light that carries hope, I am the destiny traced by myself. — replied Prosopher with his convictions.

— I don't even recognize your twinkle, I see a fog instead of glitter, the first time to witness a light that rains sparks. Aesus expressed his astonishment.

— You won't interpret what I've become, but it was necessary for me to renew myself. — said Prosopher directly.

— Be whatever you want and don't forget of kindness. — counselled Axanar.

— I don't know what had really metamorphosed. That's why I moved away, to avoid the war. — It was strange to Aesus what he had become.

— Comprehensive your way of acting, It did me good to be able to focus on what I should be doing. Thought I needed you, and in the end it was just me. I spoke of looking for you, and you ended up locating me, without looking for it, I considered you were my path, however, the path needed to go was found in me all the time. — Prosopher vented his clarity of life.

I left them and moved.

Those in chaos fed on the particles that had fallen from my fog. The spark phagocytes accompanied me, and from the height I saw Clarendel radiation attracting the phagociters.

Clarendel is located on the golden sands, far from the woods, in a desert environment, the citadel of gold, whose source of light is the Sun. All of us, of radioactive particles, feed on the Sun when it's day, and the moon when it's night, nonetheless, I lost this characteristic because of the regenerative gift of the sparkle itself, which the tree had given. Time is my friend in everything I've experienced. It accompanied my evolution, regeneration made me see that. One day, light and darkness can disappear, but time will always be there, I will never be abandoned by it.

I was inattentive between my clarifies, when I realized I already had many Algozes and Phagonellas. At first, I had no idea what to do with them, until I asked myself: what if the light controls the darkness?

— Listen! I know you're confused, hungry, fragile, crazy. There's enough light where I'm going. It will kill your hunger. — asserted Prosopher.

I'm already close to Clarendel, the city of gold and light, thirsty for actinic radiation, I control them due to the crumbs of fire. Hunger for our desires makes us vulnerable to manipulation by others.

The distance between us and the protective dome of the city reduced, outside it was the army of Claren, I think they were expecting my arrival.

"Prosopher, go away, and back to where you came!" Threatened Claren's twinkles.

— Did you spot me from afar? It is noticeable that the lights lost each other's lumetropy, if one day, you really had it. — said Prosopher ironically. Lumetropy, the term I read in the writings on the Hidden Tree.

I spread my mist, the heedless of chaos went with it, many Phagonellas were scorched by the pure light they conjure, so too, some of Claren were petrified, I resolved to end the tie, my mist petrified all of Claren. The remaining Algozes and Phagonellas gained power by absorbing the dome of light, and I drank it too, covering the whole city, leaving from being golden, turning greenish, similar to my fog. We took the upper hand, the Clarendel lights fled, and though I could have stopped them, I allowed them to get away. Most of my servants disappeared in a great searing light. The same statue I saw when my orbit was a spark killed them.

"I am Seiban, the Patron of Equilibrium. Get out or be extinct!"

I conjured the mists to attack him, however, it didn't work, the glowing hammer he carried was burning it, so he was reducing the mist that stood out from me, slowly disappearing my fog. The times I hit him, nothing happened, nevertheless, small mists entered the details of the armor and when he thought he was going to deliver the final blow, I weakened him, his internal bright, I vampirized, the armor fell, revealing the identity of a twinkle.

— You are just like me, Seiban. — said Prosopher.

— You defeated me with the kisses of your mist." Thallasus's Paragon never gave up, however, I never needed to use it to fight. I heard that the emerald fog would destroy the city, so I decided to attack you. — Replied Prosopher.

— The city holds no interest for me, yet you have created carriages without wheels that carry regimes. — said Prosopher with conviction.

— Our guidelines seek to maintain balance, if you look at natural systems, you will see. Seiban countered his criticism.

— Everything is renewed, new alignments arise in natural processes. If we stick to the systems that already exist, we'll never discover what the earth has to offer. — Prosopher revealed his ideology.

— Not all discoveries are good. — said Seiban in order to contradict him.

— Even this, a morphous light, has the highest rank in Clarendel, which I, in my seat without harm, could not."

You are hypocrites who adorn themselves as absolute truth! — Prosopher expresses his displeasure.

— It's time to put an end to this fallacy!— said Seiban, wanting to punish him with pure light.

Energy breaking out of me, I try to fight back,but it's too furious. It revived in brilliance, leaving me in the dim luminance. On Seibam's throne, the glory of the sun sat, as he prepared to scorch me once and for all, I unfolded to the throne, and he turn to me.

— Don't do that, Seiban, if you direct your power to the throne, everything in Clarendel will end! — said Prosopher, trying to convince him.

— You yourself said that everything is renewed. — Seiban uses his irony.

— It's not just us who are at stake, but the entire society of lights! Do you want to be seen as a villain? There is no villain in our story. — asked Prosopher desperately.

I managed to convince him to reduce his potency. I saw the opportunity to emit the dark in tentacles that lengthened. The remaining Phagonellas sucked light from him, even though he tried to defend himself, we beat him, my sparkle was restored. I equalized the aspects of everyone, without excluding him, keeping their brightness level.

"I accept my failure to defend Clarendal. Perhaps you are right, you should take the throne for yourself, Emerald."
Said Seiban resignedly.

— My seat I already have, the Shining Sanctuary. — Prosopher declined the offer.

— What will you do? Back where you came from? — Seiban asked out of curiosity.

The silence take me, seeing the armor, making the fog gather its pieces, it formed in me, and the gold crumbled granting a new color, Seiban named me the Emerald of Tomorrow, the new order of the world. I'm the color of the trees, armored and a mist encircling me, protector of the shrine, yet that's not what I want. I wish to persist in watching over the dusky from the light, making them always agree.

Now I have an idea of what it is to walk, in fact, I float, nonetheless, the armor walks, for being humanoid, I, inside it, am the flame of its movement, before that, I don't really know how to walk, who knows in flesh of the trees will I feel one day the tiredness of walking?
We went to the Luminescent Garden, the city was abandoned, the purine lights I found offered shelter, some accepted, others scattered in the desert. When we arrived, many were surprised by the presence of Clarendel residents in the sanctuary.

— Did the Emerald of woodlands lose the fight? Who are you in armor that frightens the shadow of our lights? —

said Haddon.

— Haddon, it's me, Prosopher. Recognize my fog. — replied Prosopher.

— What are our enemies doing here?— Haddon protested.

— Haddon, don't you understand me? They are our allies, only at that moment they were manipulated. — said Prosopher.

— I hope it's you, Prosopher — said Haddon.

I went to the garden, delivering a message to the lightwatchers:
"We are all born from the nucleus of Thallasus, the star that originates the lights, we sprout from its points, both those of Clarendel and the sentinels, we are brothers, we are one. "Prosopher.

Not everyone received the message well, talking against me, seeing me like a twinkle that doesn't shine, I saw myself as a light that shines, but generates chaos, some got excited, a multitude of fallacies exposing divergent opinions. Suddenly one flash was made, tardily dissipating, I presume it excited to calm the confusion. When it ran out, I saw three lights:

— There's always a way out of the alleys, and if there isn't, do it. — said Aesus because I told him when we were together.

— Remember that our enlightenment will give us warning when we are lost. — said Haddon.

— I see your luminosity, even if it's blurred in your own emotions. — Axanar advised.

After listening, I felt that hope came to visit me, those I saved, one day ambiguously saved and rescued me, the word of someone who enlightens is capable of saving any misguided soul, inde– pendently of where or how it got lost.

The fog decided to enter through the tiny openings in the armor, causing these crevices to enlarge. I went up, like a shooting star hurled back to where it came from. During the course I realized the distance traveled, so I threw the armor on the surface, it split, each piece falling in any surroundings; At sea, in the woods, on a glacier, on a volcano, on golden sands, the hammer fell· near my backyard, although I don't remember where.

I descended in a mist covering the botany, before gliding, the mist was already reaching them, like an inspiring and calming breeze, catching everyone.

"This act is the symbol of our friendship, I am not from Clarendel, but from the Sanctuary, although this reason does not prevent me from treating everyone the same."

— We can choose many things and one of them is love. We are stronger when we are united and weaker when we are apart. Which side do you prefer? From weakness? Or make our tabernacle a fortress? — Prosopher spoke sincerely

Finally they listened to me, staying quiet and calm, one of the abilities of nebula is to tranquilize feelings.
— Prosopher I am proud of you. — said the Elder.

— Elder Tree, would you speak again?—said Prosopher in surprise.

— Your glory influenced me to speak, extraordinary are your heights. — Eldest praises him.

— I would be nothing without your advice. I used the duskiness to my advantage, then turned it into light. — Prosopher thanked the Elder Tree.

Who knew that the dark horde would make me conquer peace, there are dark ones that are essential, I questioned myself several times darkened, and the dark always wanting to deliver answers.

I lost control to see myself masked as an enemy, since he held the necessary explanations, my biggest fear is myself, facing me at a time when there is only myself, it's impossible to escape from you. I am a living star that announces the return of light when night falls, there is no way to escape the brightness of a star at night, not even the star itself.

No matter how pure a spark is, it must care for the shadow of your light, or it will be taken over by it.

We are walkers, even if not all of us are leg walkers, trees blooming in their own ways, flowers that love their petals and their authenticity, fireflies that shine in those that are darkened from their natural shine.(Last sentence written by the Elder Tree).

...keep reading...

— And these were the last words written on Scroll of Luminous Woods.

— Is this all about the Emerald of Tomorrow?

— Yes, but it was enough to mess up your institutions.

— Aesus, I am the foundation of the doctrine that governs this world. Now that I know of his works, he won't still unpunished, like layman describes himself with your weakness.

— Your weaknesses described for anyone to read, he must have forgotten that knowledge is a weapon. Long Night Watcher restore the

naturalness of the yards, the world no longer knows who he is.

— I'll do that. No wonder I'm here.

Thus ends the tale of the Scroll of luminous wood, written by the Elder Walker.

Prosopher, I am the voice that blows in your light, you can summon me, and I will still forbid to be visible...

Glossary

Sparklife: Fire, spark, scintilla. In the language of lights, it is the affinity of a spark and the life of it.

Lumetropy: In the language of lights it means philantropy, altruism, benevolence, empathy.

Eye-bright: Iris of light, eyes.

Lightwander: Wander

Firefly: Sentinels, lightwatchers, Guardians, Lamps, Watch-lamps, Vigilantes

Notes

About the type.

This book was written in the typeface Elsie, by designers Alejandro Inler and Ana Sanfelippo, sensitive, attractive characters with their own personality. The other was Trajan, which refers to Roman inscriptions and their visual styles of typography; the letters refer to Trajan's column, which explains its sophistication, designed by Carol Twombly in 1989 and Robert Slimbach.